ICE CREAM SUMMER

STORY AND PICTURES BY

PETER SÍS

SCHOLASTIC PRESS · NEW YORK

A NOTE FROM THE AUTHOR

I had a lot of fun researching the flavorful history of ice cream. I have done my best to follow the documented facts and to connect them in this colorful story for young readers. In some cases I had to choose among the bountiful legends and varying versions. Sometimes experiments with ice cream (such as how to make it and what ingredients to include) were happening at the same time in different parts of the world. Sometimes opinions differed about ice cream inventions (such as who of the roughly fifty ice cream vendors at one world's fair was the true inventor of the sugar cone). For those interested in learning the whole scoop on this cornucopia of ice cream information, there are many wonderful books and articles you can consult. Below are a few that were helpful to me. Enjoy!

Ice Cream Cones for Sale! by Elaine Greenstein
  (Arthur A. Levine Books / Scholastic Inc., 2003)
Everybody Loves Ice Cream: The Whole Scoop on America's Favorite Treat by Shannon Jackson Arnold
  (Emmis Books, 2004)
The Great American Ice Cream Book by Paul Dickson
  (Atheneum, 1972)
Extraordinary Origins of Everyday Things by Charles Panati
  (Perennial Library / Harper & Row, 1987)

I, Italo Marchiony of New York City, patented the flat-bottomed ice cream cone in 1903, before anyone else!

Library of Congress Cataloging-in-Publication Control Number: 2014025155
ISBN 978-0-545-73161-4
10 9 8 7 6 5 4 3 2 1   15 16 17 18 19
Printed in China 38   First edition, June 2015

Book design by David Saylor and Charles Kreloff

Dear Grandpa,
Thank you for your letter.

So far, it's been
a delicious summer.

I am very busy.

But don't worry, I am not forgetting about school. I read every day.

**I am conquering big words like
tornado and _explosion_!**

I write a lot.

I am even creating my own book.

10 Scoops

+ 3 Scoops = ?

I practice my math facts.

Sometimes I trip over a simple equation.
But if I slow down, I always get it right.

Word problems are never a problem for me.
I work them out on my own . . .

. . . and with the family.

**At day camp, my friends and I study
all sorts of fascinating things.**

Today we learned cartography.
That means how to make a map.

We take exciting field trips, too,

and explore lots of new places.

You can be sure my brain is still working.
I am reading the encyclopedias you gave me.

I am diving into world history!

2,000 years ago: First ice cream

3. Rice

5. Mix it!   6. Pound it!   7. Squish it!

I am traveling to ancient China . . .

1. Snow

2. Milk

4. Fruit

8. Serve it!

Marco Polo travels the Silk Road...

...and brings recipes from China to Italy.

500-700 years ago

... and researching the whole

European continent!

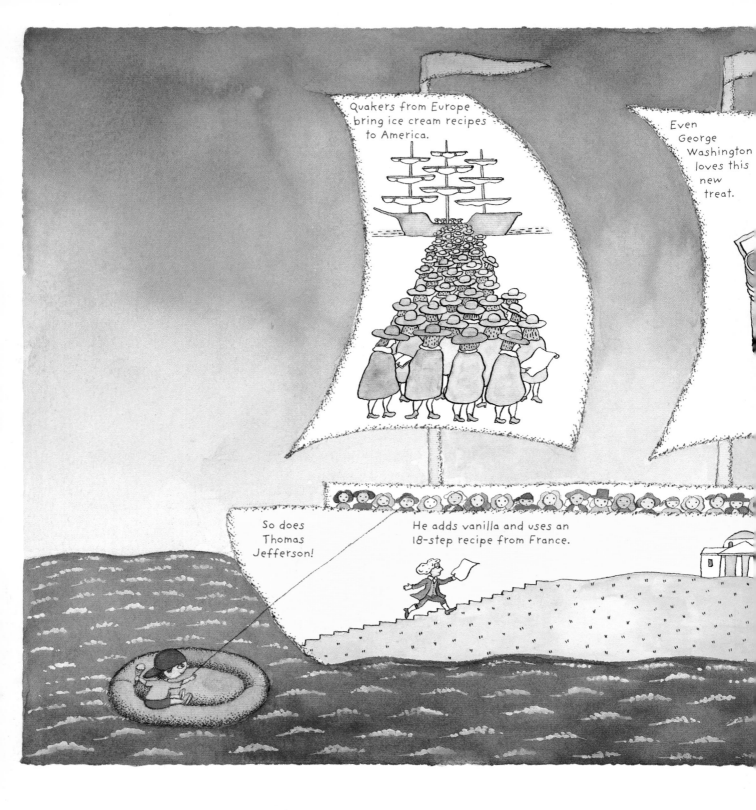

And I wouldn't forget American history.

The Founding Fathers and I have a lot in common!

St. Louis, 1904

At the World's Fair, Frenchman Arnold Fomachou *sells* ice cream.

Ernest Hamwi sells Syrian zalibia, or waffles. Arnold runs out of paper cups.

Ernest provides waffles to wrap ice cream.

The first pointy-bottomed ice cream cones are born!

I am discovering great inventors, too.

Ohio, 1920

Harry Burt experiments with dipping vanilla ice cream into melted chocolate.

Ice cream on sticks

are born!

And dreaming up some inventions of my own.

**As you can see, Grandpa, I've been
working hard all summer
(though I always take a break on sundaes).**

**I have *definitely* earned the special
trip you mentioned. I can't wait to find
out where we are going!**

To the top of Ice Cream Peak?

Wow! This is the best summer ever!